The author and publisher are indebted to James McCracken, B.D.S. (University of Glasgow) and Diane Melvin, child psychologist, for their invaluable help in the preparation of this book.

First published in 1989 by Conran Octopus Limited
This edition first published in Britain in 2002 by Brimax,
an imprint of Octopus Publishing Group Ltd
2-4 Heron Quays, London E14 4JP

**McGraw-Hill
Children's Publishing**

This edition published in the United States in 2002 by
McGraw-Hill Children's Publishing,
a Division of The McGraw-Hill Companies
8787 Orion Place
Columbus, OH 43240

www.MHkids.com

Printed in China.

1-57768-987-9

Library of Congress Cataloging-in-Publication Data is on file with the publisher.

1 2 3 4 5 6 7 8 9 BRI 07 06 07 05 04 03 02

The **McGraw-Hill** Companies

First Experiences

Danny Goes to the Dentist

Written by **Robert Robinson**

Illustrated by **Nicola Smee**

McGraw-Hill
Children's Publishing
Columbus, Ohio

It's almost time for bed. Mom is reading Danny and Emma a book all about teeth. Tomorrow, they are going to visit their dentist, Dr. Clark.

The dentist isn't far from their house, so they walk to the office.

"We've come for a check-up," Mom tells the lady behind the desk.

The waiting room is full of people. Danny sees his friend, Matthew. They play cars together while they wait. Mom reads Emma a story.

Soon Dr. Clark's assistant, the hygienist, comes to take Danny and Emma to the exam room. Mom comes with them.

"Hello, you two," Dr. Clark says. "How are you?"
"I have a new tooth," says Danny, proudly.
"That's great," says Dr. Clark. "Soon you'll lose other teeth and get new ones in their place."

"Now then, who wants to be first?" he asks.
"Me please," says Emma.

The hygienist ties a bib around Emma's neck.
"What is the bib for?" Emma asks.
"It is to keep your clothes from getting wet," says the hygienist.

"This is a very comfortable chair," says Emma. "It's a special chair," says Dr. Clark. He pushes a button, and soon Emma's chair is tilted back.

"How are your teeth?" asks Dr. Clark.
"They are fine, thank you," Emma replies.
"Let's have a look," he says. "Open wide."

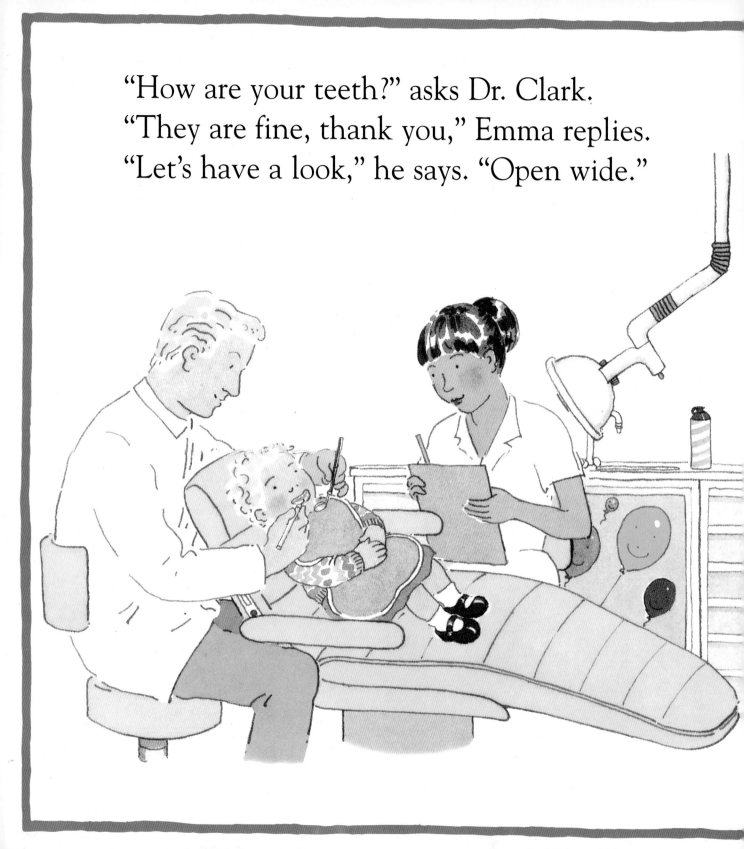

Dr. Clark gently checks Emma's teeth with a thin, pointed instrument. Then, he uses a small mirror on a stick to see her top teeth.

"Your teeth look fine," says Dr. Clark. "Now I'll polish them to make them extra clean."
The brush tickles Emma's mouth. The paste tastes like mint.

"Your turn now, Danny," says Dr. Clark. "I want to see your new tooth." Danny climbs into the chair and opens his mouth wide.

The dentist looks at all of Danny's teeth.
He tells the hygienist what he sees and she writes
down some notes.

"Don't forget his new tooth," says Emma.

Dr. Clark finds a hole, or cavity, in one of Danny's teeth.

"I think that you have been eating too much candy," he says. "I am going to clean out the tooth a little with my drill and put in a filling for you. It will stop the hole from becoming larger."

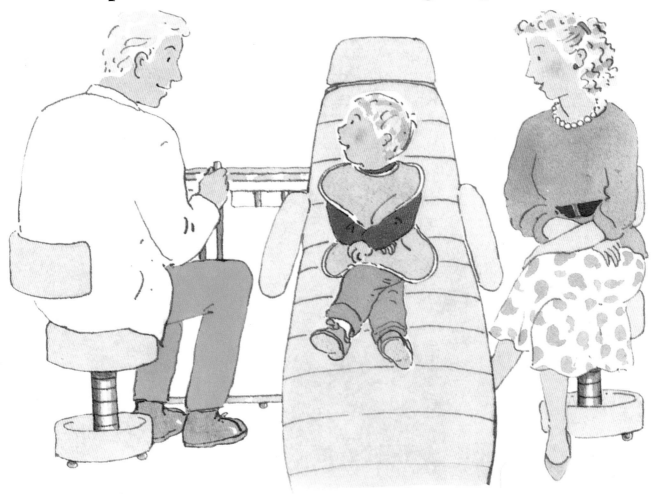

Before Dr. Clark uses the drill, he gives Danny a shot to numb his tooth. The drill makes a rumbling noise but it doesn't hurt Danny.

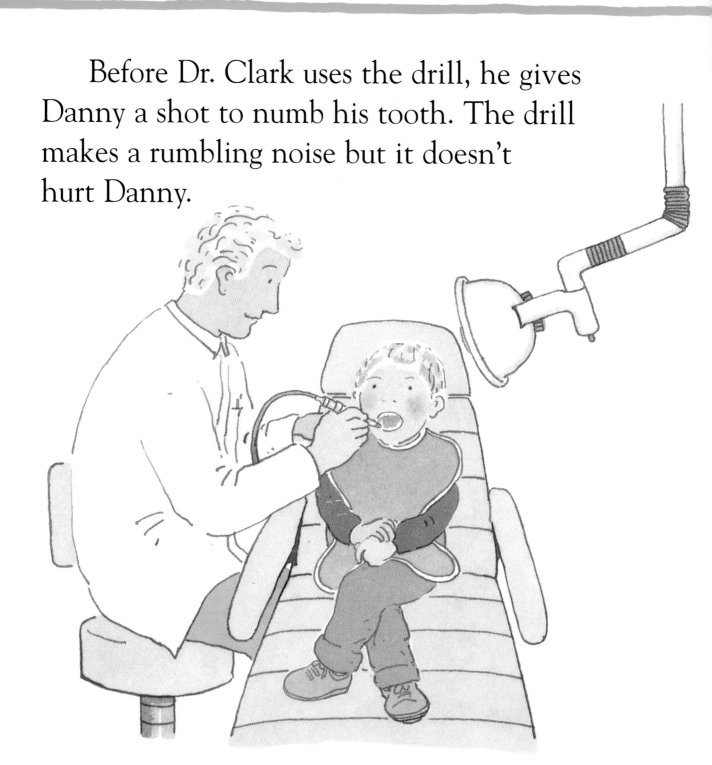

The hygienist makes a filling mixture that looks like white toothpaste. Dr. Clark fills Danny's tooth with it.

"Leave your mouth open for a minute while this hardens," he says.

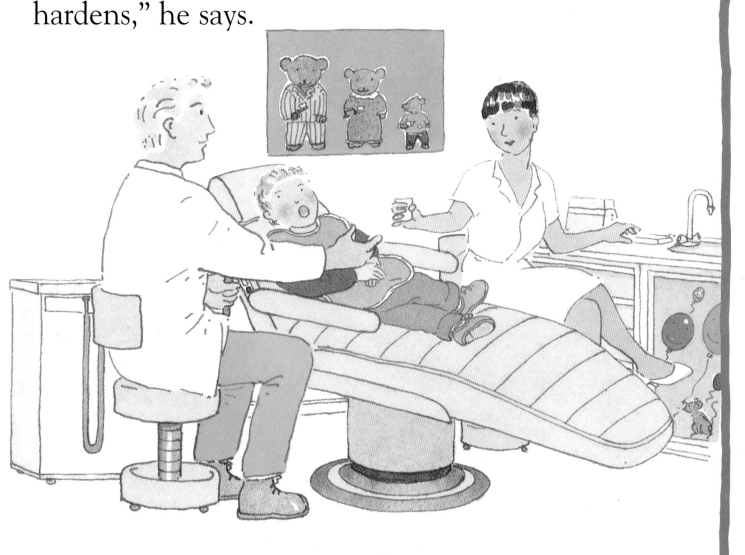

When the tooth is ready, Danny takes a sip of mouthwash. He swishes it around his mouth and spits into a funnel.

"All done," says Dr. Clark. "Now remember to take good care of your teeth. You need to brush and floss them twice a day. Flossing will clean the food out from between your teeth." He gives Danny and Emma a poster and two balloons.

"Try not to eat too many sweets, either," he says.

On the way out, the lady behind the desk lets Emma and Danny each choose a sticker and a toothbrush.

At bedtime, they use their new toothbrushes. Then, they floss their teeth to remove every bit of food.

Mom puts up the poster in their room.
"I hope that if I eat what this says, I will never need another filling," Danny says.

Eat these for treats—not sticky sweets